Let's Play
TAG!

 Read the Page

Read the Story

Game

Yes   No

Repeat

Stop

D1025157

"Come on guys, we all knew this day was coming," Woody says, as the toys prepare to be stored in the attic.

"Andy isn't a kid anymore. He's going off to college."

DONATE

DELIVER TO
EMERYVILLE

Disney · PIXAR

TOY
STORY
3

TOGETHER
again

illustrated by
Estudi Iboix

1

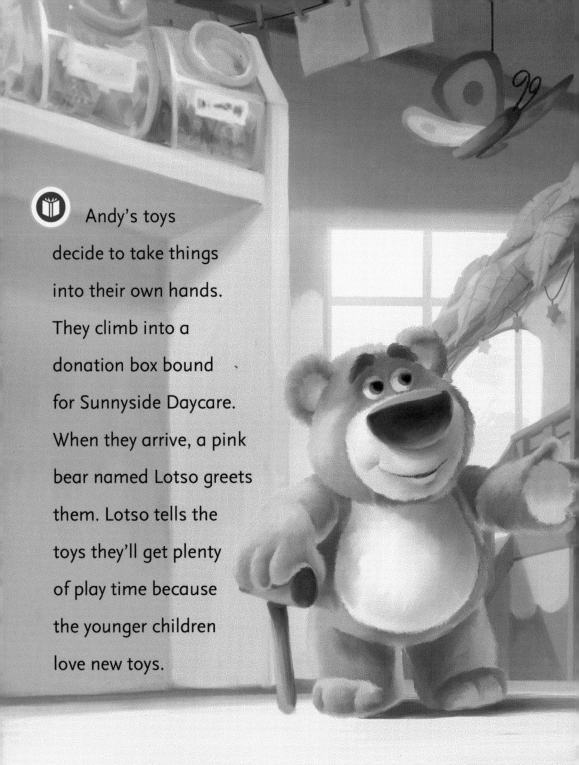

Andy's toys decide to take things into their own hands. They climb into a donation box bound for Sunnyside Daycare. When they arrive, a pink bear named Lotso greets them. Lotso tells the toys they'll get plenty of play time because the younger children love new toys.

But Woody wants to be with Andy. He tries to leave, but things don't go quite as planned, and a little girl named Bonnie finds him.

The rest of the toys decide to stay.

The toddlers in the Caterpillar Room play too roughly with Andy's toys.

SNAP!

They won't last a week in this place!

"There's been some mistake," says
Buzz. "I'll talk to Lotso."

SMASH!

Buzz finds Lotso. Instead of helping, Lotso flips a switch on Buzz's back. Now Buzz thinks his friends are agents of the evil Emperor Zurg!

Back in the Caterpillar Room,
Buzz stands guard. "Prisoners disabled,
Commander Lotso," he reports.
Lotso grins. With Buzz working for Lotso,
who will rescue Andy's toys?

Meanwhile, in
Bonnie's room, Woody
is having a great time.

If only all of Andy's toys could be there!
He tells Trixie and her friends about the
pink bear he met at Sunnyside.
Bonnie's toys gasp when they
hear Lotso's name.

They tell Woody that Lotso
is plush and huggable on
the outside, but inside
he's mean.

Woody can't believe it.
**"I have to rescue
my friends!"**

Woody sneaks
his way back
into Sunnyside.

He finds his friends and together they make a
plan to escape. Woody is determined.

"We've got to stick together so we can bust out of here tonight!"

"First, we turn off the security monitors!"
says Woody.

Slinky Dog helps Woody shut the monitors down. Without them, Lotso won't be able to see what Woody and the gang are doing!

Now to fix Buzz.

Woody finds a Buzz Lightyear manual.
"Quick, open his back! There's a switch!"
Woody says.

But resetting Buzz doesn't
do quite what he expected.

RANGER

LIGHTYEAR

15

"¿Habeis visto mi nave espacial?" says Buzz.

Oh no! The toys accidentally switched Buzz into Spanish mode. Time is running short. Woody directs the toys, "Come on! The trash chute—it's our only way out."

The toys slide down the chute into the dumpster.

But Lotso and his crew are waiting for them and block the escape route. Lotso tells the toys to play by his rules or it's off to the dump.

Suddenly, a garbage truck pulls up and lifts the dumpster.

The toys **TUMBLE** into darkness.

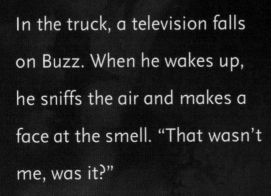

In the truck, a television falls on Buzz. When he wakes up, he sniffs the air and makes a face at the smell. "That wasn't me, was it?"

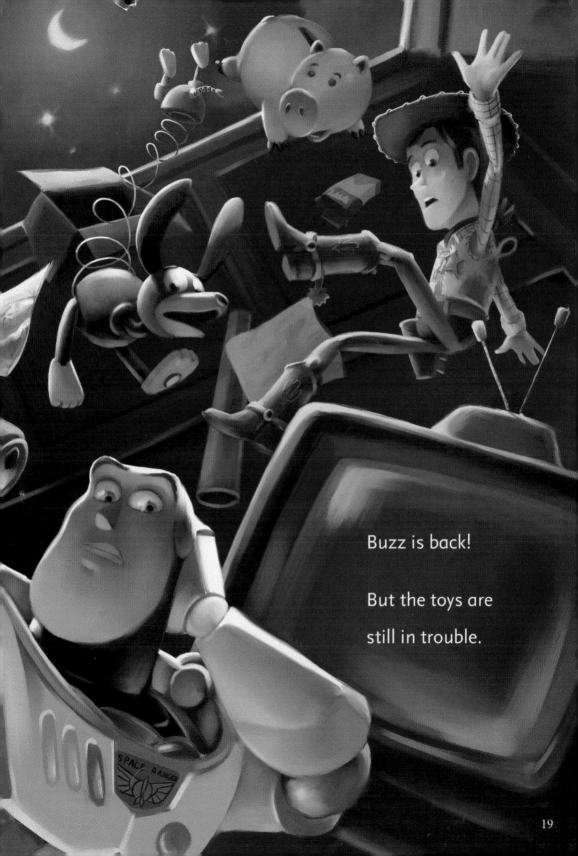

Buzz is back!

But the toys are
still in trouble.

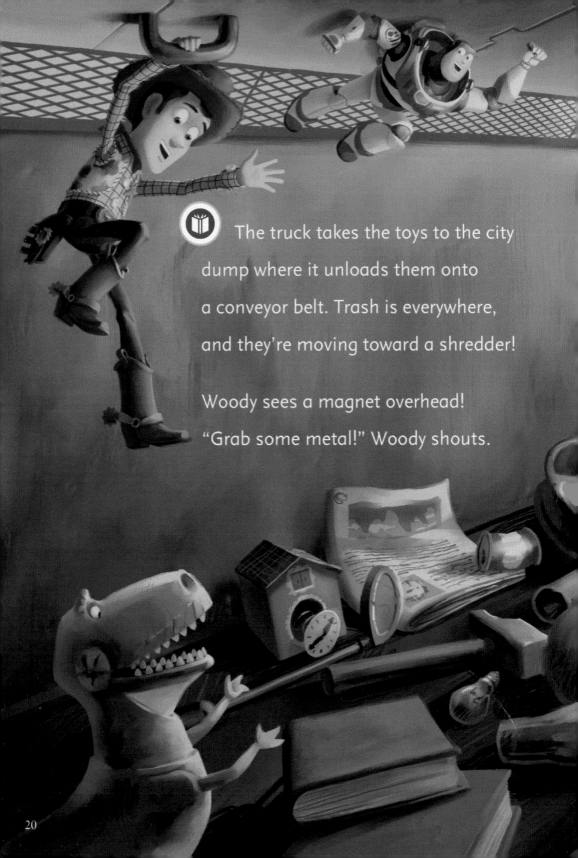

The truck takes the toys to the city dump where it unloads them onto a conveyor belt. Trash is everywhere, and they're moving toward a shredder!

Woody sees a magnet overhead! "Grab some metal!" Woody shouts.

The toys fly up to the magnet, only to find that the metal is heading toward a big fire!

"Run!" Woody yells.

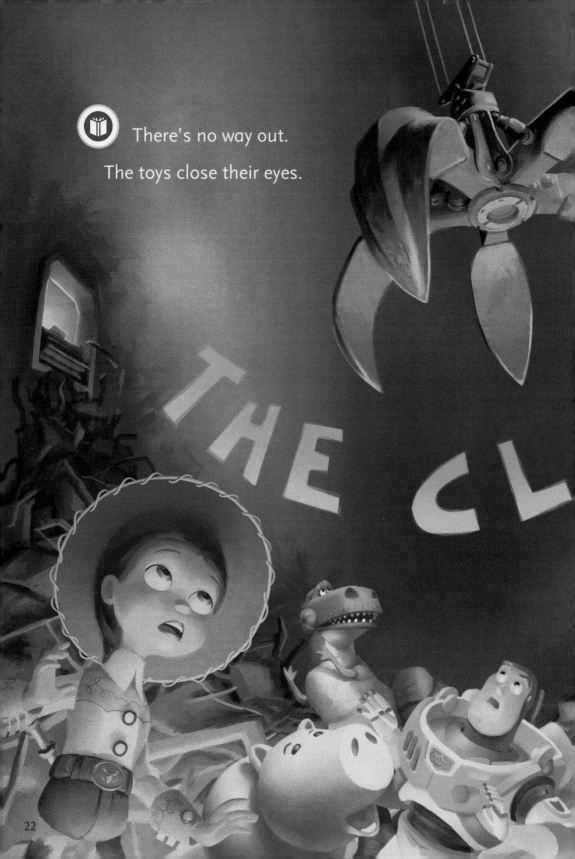

There's no way out.

The toys close their eyes.

It's the alien toys to the rescue!

"C'mon, guys," says Woody.

"Let's go home."

23

At Andy's house, the toys get ready to go
to the attic. But Woody has another idea.
He writes something new on the box.
Seeing Woody's note, Andy delivers
the toys to Bonnie's house. His toys
will be happy there.

Buzz and Woody watch
Andy's car drive away.

"So long, partner," Woody says softly.

He turns to Buzz.

"Whatever happens,
at least we're together."

Buzz answers, "To infinity and beyond."

BONNIE'S playtime

ALIEN *invasion*